"I was born in London in 1946 and grew up in a sweet shop in Essex. For several years I worked as a graphic designer, but in 1980 I decided to concentrate on writing and illustrating books for children.

My wife, Annette, and I have two grown-up children, Ben and Amanda, and we have put down roots in Suffolk.

I haven't recently counted how many books there are with my name on the cover but Percy the Park Keeper accounts for a good many of them. I'm reliably informed that they have sold more than three million copies. Hooray!

I didn't realise this when I invented Percy, but I can now see that he's very like my mum's dad, my grandpa. I even have a picture of him giving a ride to my brother and me in his old home-made wooden wheelbarrow!"

NICK BUTTERWORTH

PERCY'S FRIENDS
THE MICE

NICK BUTTERWORTH

Collins

An imprint of HarperCollinsPublishers

Thanks Graham Daldry. You're a wizard.

Thanks Atholl McDonald. You're a hero!

First published in Great Britain by HarperCollins Publishers Ltd in 2001

1 3 5 7 9 10 8 6 4 2

ISBN: 0 00 711979 8

Text and illustrations copyright © Nick Butterworth 2001
The author asserts the moral right to be identified as the author of the work.

The HarperCollins website address is: www.**fire**and**water**.com

Printed and bound in Belgium

MY FRIENDS THE MICE

Always busy, always fun, and always *there*. The mice get into my pockets and even into my boots! And there always seems to be at least one mouse sitting on top of my cap.

The mice are not very brave, but that is probably because they are so small.

Actually, the mice can be very helpful. Their sharp eyes and ears notice all sorts of things that I would miss. And their nimble fingers are extremely good at untying difficult knots!

I like to look after them and make sure that they don't get forgotten or left out, just because they're little.

Can you imagine what it would be like to be as small as a mouse? Here are two mice by the wheel of my wheelbarrow.

My friendly old wheelbarrow looks much more scary when you look at it the way they see it. Watch your tail, little mouse!

By the way, that black lump is part of one of my boots!

THE MICE REALLY LIKE . . .

Chocolate! I thought it was the fox who had been eating my Easter egg. I was wrong!

Cheering people up. They brought this daffodil for me when I was feeling poorly.

THE MICE DON'T LIKE . . .

Cats. Especially big ones!

Snowball fights. Well, not with big
snowballs anyway!

Being so small, the mice
can't join in when the other
animals play with a ball.
That doesn't bother them.
   With two plastic spoons and
         a few peas, they have all they need
                  for a game of mouse tennis!

I've got lots of pictures in my photo album.

Goodness! Is it that time already? Seventeen o'clock!

How much fun could you have with a cotton reel and a piece of old washing line?

Here are some I took of my good friends, the mice.

A cosy place for a ride in winter. And if it snows, you might find them in the fox's ears!

A tin bath makes a perfect swimming pool for mice!

When I lost a button from my trousers, I asked the mice to help me find it. They searched and searched all over my hut.

In the end, they found three buttons, a
safety pin, a conker and a small key.
I don't remember losing the key.
 The strange thing was, that none of
the buttons were from my trousers.

Here's a jolly little song that the mice like to sing when they ride on my cap. It can be a skipping rhyme too...

WE'RE MICE!

We're not very tall. We're not big at all.
In fact, we are small...We're mice!

We love to eat cheese. We never get fleas.
We always say please...We're mice!

We never would chat to a cat or a rat,
Or a bat, come to that...We're mice!

We all like to nap on Percy's cap.
He's such a nice chap...We're mice!

Whenever it's snowing, our ears will start glowing,
To show where we're going...We're mice!

We hope you can see and agree that all we
Are as nice as can be...We're mice!

FAVOURITE PLACES

There are lots of mice and
they all have their own
favourite places.

I know one who likes to be out on a boat.
As long as the water isn't too choppy, that is.
Another of the mice
likes to play in a
deserted bird's nest.
I hope the bird
doesn't want it back.

One little mouse likes to curl up for
a sleep in my socks. Clean
ones, of course.

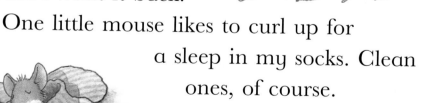

Another seems to think that my sandwich
box is the best place to be!

One mouse used to
like to play in an old
watering can. He liked
the way it made his voice
sound big! He stopped
playing in it after he got
stuck in the spout.

There's one mouse who says, "There's no
place like home." I think they all feel that
really. I do too, don't you? Home for
the mice is in the big tree house...

Here they are, working hard as usual, at the very important business of enjoying themselves! My friends the mice.

THE TREE HOUSE

In this picture you'll see Percy the Park Keeper and his friends. But if you look very carefully, you can also find a balloon, a kite, a hot-water bottle, a model aeroplane, a paintbrush, a robin, a beach ball, a magpie, a yo-yo, Percy's stripy mug, a pencil, a conker, Percy's watering can, a cheese roll, a framed picture of Percy, one of Percy's gardening gloves, a model yacht, a plastic duck, a banana, and a frog. Oh, and ten ladybirds!

FREE GIANT POSTER

Nick Butterworth's new, giant picture of the tree house
in Percy's Park shows Percy and all his animal friends
in and around their tree house home. There are also
lots of things hidden in the picture. Some are easy
to find. Some are much harder!

To send off for your free poster, simply snip off
FOUR tokens, each from a different book in the
Percy the Park Keeper and his Friends series and send them
to the address below. Remember to include
your name, address and age.

Percy Poster, Children's Marketing Department,
Harper Collins Publishers, 77-85 Fulham Palace Road, London W6 8JB

Offer applies to UK and Eire only. Available while stocks last.
Allow 28 days for delivery.

Read all the stories about Percy and his animal friends...

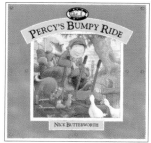

Percy toys and videos
are also available.